"I think Puddle is really clever and naughty, but nice, and I loved it when he made the pirate captain walk the plank. I like Ruby and Harry. I think they are funny and brave and very good at having adventures. I liked the pirates because they were nice pirates."
Maeve, age 6

"I thought Puddle was a very cheeky puppy and the more mischief he got into the more I laughed! The part when they had the hiccups was so funny that it almost made me hiccup myself!"
Carmen, age 6

Pirate Surprise

Other books about
Puddle the Naughtiest Puppy:

Puddle
the naughtiest puppy

Pirate Surprise

by Hayley Daze
illustrated by David Opie
cover illustrated by Paul Hardman

A catalogue record for this book is available from the British Library

Published by Ladybird Books Ltd MMX
A Penguin Company
Penguin Books Ltd., 80 Strand, London WC2R 0RL, UK
Penguin Books Australia Ltd., Camberwell, Victoria, Australia
Penguin Group (NZ) 67 Apollo Drive, Rosedale,
North Shore 0632, New Zealand

1 3 5 7 9 10 8 6 4 2
Series created by Working Partners Limited, London W6 0QT
Text © Working Partners Ltd MMX
Cover illustration © Working Partners Ltd MMX
Interior illustrations © Ladybird Books Ltd MMX

Special thanks to Mo O' Hara

ISBN: 978-1-40930-404-3
Printed in England

For Hugo, Freddie, Gabe, Mark and David –
my Nephew Pirate Posse

When clouds fill the sky and rain starts to fall,
Ruby and Harry are not sad at all.
They know that when puddles appear on the ground,
A magical puppy will soon be around!

Puddle's his name, and he's the one
Who can lead you to worlds of adventure and fun!
He may be quite naughty, but he's clever too,
So come follow Puddle – he's waiting for you!

A present from Puddle:

Look out for the special code at the back of the book to
get extra-special games and loads of free stuff at Puddle's
website! Come and play at www.puddlethepuppy.com

Contents

Chapter One
Adventure Ahoy!

"*Brrp brrp, brrp brrp, brrp brrp, brrrrrrrrp!*" Ruby blew through the reeds she had pressed between her thumbs, making a trumpet sound.

"Announcing Queen Ruby!" she shouted. Her voice echoed around Grandad's pond.

"What about me?" Harry asked. He smiled and gazed proudly at the model sailing ship he was holding.

"Ooops. Sorry," Ruby said and then shouted, "and announcing the Queen's Master Ship Builder, Harry!"

The cousins' wellies squelched in the mud as they marched to the pond's edge and set the ship down. Harry took out his compass and unrolled the map of the pond that he had made earlier.

"We are ready to launch the boat," Ruby said in her best queenly voice.

"She's a ship," Harry said.

"Who's a ship?" Ruby asked.

"My model, she's a sea-going ship. Not a boat," Harry explained. "Ships are bigger and have three or more masts. Just remember, a boat can fit in a ship, but a ship can't fit in a boat."

"But yours can fit in a bathtub?" Ruby rolled her eyes. "Never mind. We are ready to launch the ship. Now for the fun bit where we christen it with the bottle." Ruby held up a bottle of fizzy drink, shook it and started to unscrew the lid.

"Wait!" Harry exclaimed. "I need to check the course one more time." He scanned his map.

Splat! A large drop of rain plopped on to the map. Then another drop fell, and another. The pond was now rippling with raindrops.

Ruby and Harry shouted together, "Hooray, it's raining!"

Come on Puddle, Ruby thought. *Where will we go this time?* They scouted around for Puddle but there was no sign of the naughty puppy.

Puddle magically appeared whenever it started raining and took Ruby and Harry on amazing adventures.

Oh no! Maybe he's not coming? Ruby wondered.

Suddenly they heard a rustling in the reeds behind them, and *whoomp* – out bounded Puddle, leaping high into the air above the pond.

"Woof!" Puddle yipped as he landed in the water with a terrific splash. The wave he made pushed Harry's ship on to the mud and soaked the cousins through. Ruby slipped and her thumb knocked against the lid of the fizzy drink bottle, which was still in her hand.

"Ooops!" she squealed as it popped its lid and sprayed all over Harry.

"Yuck!" Harry said, wiping his sticky glasses.

"Naughty Puddle," Ruby said through her laughter. "You scared us and you could have sunk Harry's ship!"

Puddle leapt out of the pond and started to shake himself dry.

"Puddle!" Harry shouted as his glasses got splashed once more.

Puddle ran in and out of Harry's legs and wagged his tail.

"At least the water washed off the fizzy drink," Ruby said, giggling.

Harry smiled at the playful puppy. "You are the naughtiest puppy I know. Oh no, my map." Harry held up the soggy paper. He put the compass safely in his pocket.

Puddle yapped and dashed down Grandad's garden path. He scampered among the puddles, then circled a large one near the garden gate. Ruby and Harry raced over.

"I guess this is the one," Ruby said, getting ready to hop into it with

Puddle. "Come on. Let's all go together this time," she suggested, holding out her hand to Harry.

"Are you sure we'll fit?" Harry asked.

Ruby gripped his hand and tugged on her plaits for luck. "There's only one way to find out."

"OK," Harry said. He took a deep breath. "Here goes!"

And they all jumped into the puddle and disappeared with an enormous splash.

Chapter Two
A Scary Surprise

Ruby landed with a thud on a wooden floor.

A split second later, Harry landed on top of her with a slightly softer thud.

Then Puddle landed gently on top with hardly a thud at all. "Ruff," he yelped as he bounced on to the floor.

Ruby wiggled from under Harry

and rolled over on to her back. She stared up at the blue sky. "It looks like the sky is rocking back and forth, but we're standing still," she said.

"My stomach feels kind of funny, like it did when we were on the flying carpet. Hey, maybe we're flying again," Harry said.

The cousins scrambled to their
feet. They were standing in what
seemed to be a big wooden bucket.
They peered over the side, and their
mouths dropped open when they saw
what was below them – sails, ropes
and men running about on deck.

"A boat!" Ruby said. "We're in the lookout thingy of a boat!"

"A ship!" Harry said, smiling. "And the thingy is called the crow's nest."

Ruby and Harry gazed at the sails billowing around them. The wind grew stronger and the flag above their heads unfurled.

"Wow, Puddle," Ruby said, patting the puppy on the head. "I wonder what kind of ship it is."

Harry tugged on Ruby's sleeve to get her attention. "I think I know," he said.

Ruby turned as Harry pointed to the flag flying above them. It was black with a white skull and crossbones – the Jolly Roger!

"Pirates?" Ruby said, squealing with excitement. "We're on a pirate ship!" Then she paused and looked at the flag again. Her smile faded away. "Oh, no. We're on a real pirate ship – with real pirates."

The cousins ducked back down in the crow's nest.

"We've got to get out of here," Ruby said.

"Come on, Puddle, let's go back home now," Harry said.

Ruby got up and tried to make Puddle chase her around the crow's nest.

"If I can just get him to run in circles around us, then that will take us home," she said. "That's how it's always worked before – everything goes fuzzy, and then *poof*, we're back in Grandad's garden."

But Puddle wouldn't budge. He sat gently scratching at the wooden sides of the crow's nest and whimpering at Ruby.

"Do you want to see, boy? Is that it?" Ruby said, scooping up the puppy. Puddle licked Ruby's face as they peeked out over the side.

"Harry, you have to see this," Ruby whispered. She put Puddle down and tried to pull Harry to his feet.

"I don't need to see any scary pirates," Harry said, covering his eyes.

"It's not the pirates I'm worried about," Ruby replied.

Harry slowly stood and uncovered his eyes. He gasped. The ocean in front of them was spinning in a huge whirlpool.

"It's a maelstrom," Harry said, his eyes wide with disbelief.

"A what?" Ruby asked.

"A very powerful whirlpool," Harry explained.

Ruby thought it looked like the sea was whirling in a giant milkshake machine.

"Whatever you call it," Ruby said, her voice trembling, "we're heading right for it!"

Chapter Three
Look Out Below!

"We have to tell someone about the whirlpool," Ruby said, staring at the swirling water.

"Do you know what pirates do to stowaways?" Harry asked. "You know, people who come on to their ship uninvited."

Ruby imagined walking the plank blindfolded with Harry and Puddle, while sharks circled beneath them. She shook her head to get rid of the image.

"OK, maybe that's not a great idea," Ruby muttered. "I'm sure the pirates will see the whirlpool in time to steer around it."

"Of course," Harry said. "That's why they put sailors as lookouts up in the crow's nest."

They both gulped as they realized that they were the only ones in the crow's nest – so the ship didn't have any lookouts.

"Woof, woof!" Puddle barked.

"Shhhhh – the pirates will hear us," Ruby whispered as she and Harry crouched down again. "Naughty Puddle."

"Woof! Woof!" Puddle barked, even louder than before.

Ruby tried to grab Puddle to cover his mouth, but he wriggled away and started running around the crow's nest. He scratched and howled as the ship rocked harder from side to side.

"Ahoy, up there!" shouted a voice from the deck. "If there be stowaways aboard then show yourselves."

Harry and Ruby both took a deep breath and stood up with their arms in the air.

"We surrender," Harry said, taking out a white handkerchief from his pocket and waving it above his head.

Before Ruby or Harry could stop the puppy, Puddle leapt on to the ledge of the crow's nest and sprang into the air.

Ruby lunged towards him.

"Puddle, no!" she screamed. She leaned over the side of the crow's nest with Harry holding on tight to the hem of her dress. The ship pitched left and Ruby started to tip out.

Harry pulled Ruby back into the crow's nest as the ship lurched back again. They fell in a heap on the floor. They were safe, but where was Puddle? Ruby and Harry looked out to see the little puppy hanging off the wooden boom that held up the main sail.

"Hold on, Puddle!" Harry shouted.
Puddle wagged his tail and barked
at Harry and Ruby. Then he slid off
the boom and on to the huge white sail.
Puddle dug his claws into the fabric
as he slid down,
leaving long
gashes, until at
last he landed
on the deck.

"Puddle, you naughty puppy!" Ruby shouted. *Now the pirates are going to be really angry*, she thought.

"See what he's done," Harry said.

"I know," Ruby said. "He's ruined the big sail-sheet-whatsit so it can't puff out any more."

"Puddle has slowed down the ship," Harry explained. "With the main sail torn, the ship won't go nearly so fast."

"I get it," Ruby said, brightening. "It'll take longer to get to the whirlpool. We might still have time to warn the pirates."

"All right, you stowaways, that's one of you on the deck," a pirate in a red bandanna called to them from the deck. "Now, you two best come down the ladder."

Ruby eyed the swinging rope ladder that hung over the side of the crow's nest. "Go down there?" she gulped. "Puddle, what have you got us into now?"

Chapter Four
Yo Ho Puddle

Ruby and Harry stared down at
the pirates who were gathering on
the deck. They were a colourful
crew with bright clothes and shiny
cutlasses that glinted in the sun.

A pirate with an eye-patch laughed
and slapped his thigh. "That's gotta be
the funniest thing I ever seen a dog do,"
he said, patting Puddle on the head.

The other pirates laughed.

Harry turned to Ruby, his brow creased in confusion. "The pirates don't seem very cross, do they?" he asked.

"They might be when they see the whirlpool," Ruby replied.

Puddle ran to the bottom of the ladder and yelped.

"We're coming, Puddle," shouted Ruby. She took a deep breath. The pirates were clustered around the bottom of the ladder. But she had no choice – she had to get to Puddle. She started to climb down.

Harry had just climbed on to the ladder as well when the ship lurched to one side, making the ladder swing to the right.

"The sea's getting rougher the closer we get to the whirlpool," Harry yelled to Ruby.

Then the ship pitched to the left
and the ladder swung again. This
time Ruby lost her grip on the
rope and her hands slid off.
As she fell back,
she tightened her
knees around a
rung of the ladder
and caught herself,
as if she was hanging
upside down on a
set of monkey bars.

"I'm OK!" she
shouted to Harry, her
plaits swinging in the
air. "But the ladder's
moving too much!"

Puddle yowled at the pirates and grabbed hold of the bottom of the ladder with his teeth. To Ruby's surprise, a few of the pirates held on too, and the ladder stopped swinging. Ruby pulled herself the right way up and scrambled down.

Harry followed right behind her.

"Thanks, Puddle," Ruby said, giving the puppy a big hug.

"Thank you, pirates," Harry said, pushing his glasses up the bridge of his nose. "I mean, sailors, or um, gentlemen?"

"Pirates will do us fine, won't it, ye motley crew?" said the pirate with a patch over his eye.

The whole crew shouted, "Aye!"

"This is Patch and you can call me Olly," the pirate with the bandanna said, stepping forward. He wore a bright waistcoat and a leather holster, which held a telescope instead of a pistol.

He's not much older than us, thought Ruby.

"Thanks, Olly," she said aloud,

shaking his hand. "Are you the captain?"

Olly smiled. "I'm the first mate. And the youngest first mate of any pirate ship that sails the high seas. Who are you?"

"I'm Ruby," Ruby said, "and this is my cousin Harry." Puddle hopped down from her arms. "Oh, and this is Puddle."

"We need to speak to the captain," Harry said.

Olly and the other pirates laughed.

"No one disturbs the captain when he's asleep," Olly explained. "Not if they know what's good for them."

"But we have to tell him about the maelstrom," Harry said.

"The what?" Olly asked.

"Never mind that." Patch scratched his head and gazed up at the crow's nest. "How did ye landlubbers stow on board our ship?"

Puddle started yapping loudly and pulling on Olly's trouser leg.

"What is it, Puddle?" Olly asked.

Puddle ran to the side of the ship and yapped again, in the direction of the whirlpool.

Olly followed, took out his telescope and looked at the sea.

"Blow me down!" he shouted. "A whirlpool dead ahead. All hands on deck!"

Chapter Five
Racing the Waves

Olly ran to the ship's wheel. "Ready about," he shouted to the crew as they started to climb ropes and pull sails.

"Are you sure we shouldn't go and get the captain?" Harry asked.

"That really wouldn't help," Olly said, turning the heavy wooden wheel.

Ruby pictured how scary the captain must be if he was more terrifying than the whirlpool.

"Right, you two are now honorary members of our pirate crew," Olly said, pointing to Harry and Ruby.

"Aye, aye," the cousins answered together.

"Ruby, hoist the topsail!" Olly shouted. Ruby scanned all the sails hanging from the masts, not sure which one to hoist. Puddle sank his teeth into a rope and barked.

"That's the one, Puddle," Olly said.

Ruby grabbed hold of it and pulled with all her might until the sail reached the top of the mast and opened.

"Good. Now, Harry, splice the spinnaker rigging," Olly ordered.

"The spinach what?" Ruby asked.

"Don't worry, I know what it is. It's the big sail at the front," Harry said. He ran to the front of the ship with Ruby and Puddle right behind him.

"Hard rudder starboard!" Olly shouted to the other pirates as the ship started to turn.

"It's working!" Ruby called to Harry.

"The wind from the sails is pushing us away from the whirlpool," Harry replied. "I just hope it's fast enough."

"Someone hoist the aft sail! We need more speed!" shouted Olly.

"That's the sail at the back of the ship," said Harry.

"Come on, Puddle!" shouted Ruby. She raced to the rear deck of the ship, Puddle running at her feet. She pulled on the rope that controlled the sail and Puddle tugged it with his teeth. The aft sail opened and caught a gust of wind that pushed the pirate ship safely out of the whirlpool's pull.

"We did it, Puddle," Ruby shouted.

"We all did it, crew!" Olly said.
"And that includes our three newest
pirates!"

The pirates slid down their ropes
and ran to the centre of the ship to
celebrate.

"Ahoy, all ye pirates that follow the sea," sang Patch in a loud gravelly voice.

Puddle danced along as the crew joined in the chorus.

"Yo, ho, blow the man down!"

Suddenly the ship lurched to the right. Everyone tumbled across the deck. Puddle rolled into Ruby's legs.

"Oh no," Olly said. "We've woken the captain!" The singing stopped, and Patch and the rest of the crew headed for their posts. "You see, there's a little problem with –" Olly began to explain, but the ship rocked in the other direction.

"The steering?" Harry asked.

"You might say that," Olly replied. "I think it's time you met the captain." He led Harry, Ruby and Puddle along the shaking deck.

"But the sea's calm now," Ruby

said. "Why are we still rocking so much?"

"It's the captain's hiccups," Olly said.

"What do you mean?" Ruby asked.

"Look," Olly said as they reached the rear of the ship.

The cousins stared up at the pirate captain turning the huge wooden wheel that steered the ship. He wore a three-cornered pirate hat with a skull and crossbones at the front. With each loud hiccup, his long bushy red beard bounced and he yanked the wheel sideways, sending the ship shuddering and the crew tumbling down.

Ruby clung to the mast as the ship lurched through the water. With the hiccupping captain at the wheel, who knew where they would end up?

Chapter Six

Hiccups on the High Seas

"Why can't someone else steer?" Ruby asked, dashing to the railing and bracing herself for the next hiccup.

"When the captain is awake, no one steers the ship but him," Olly said. "Captain's orders."

"And a pirate wouldn't disobey his captain," Harry said, pointing to the plank that jutted off the edge of the ship, over the sea.

Ruby gulped and looked over the side for sharks.

The captain called out to Olly. "Arrr ... *hic* ... stowaway ... *hic* ... on me ship," he shouted.

Ruby could hardly understand what the captain was saying, but she could tell that he didn't sound happy.

"Captain Redbeard, this is Ruby, Harry and Puddle," Olly said. "They helped us steer away from the whirlpool."

"Singin' ... *hic* ... barkin' ... *hic*," Redbeard said.

"Yes, Captain, sorry the noise woke you," Olly said, backing away from the top deck.

"Where's me ... *hic* ... map?" the captain asked. "Off course ... *hic* ... again."

Olly whispered to Harry and Ruby, "It's the captain's wild steering that's got us off course. If he stays at the helm, we might end up back at the whirlpool."

The captain hiccupped again and the ship tilted to the side.

"Captain, why don't we steer for a bit?" Ruby said. "You could take a break."

"Break? Captain's place ... *hic* ... at the wheel!" Redbeard shouted.

"I think that's a 'no'," Harry whispered to Ruby.

"Then we'll have to cure Captain Redbeard of his hiccups!" she insisted.

Puddle ran over to a barrel of fresh water on deck.

"Water, that's what we need," Ruby said as she scooped up a cup of water from the barrel. She turned to Captain Redbeard. "I think we can help get rid of your hiccups. All you have to do is drink this cup of water while standing on your head."

Captain Redbeard glared at Olly and grunted. "Shiver me ... *hic* ... Better work ... *hic*."

The captain leaned over and
carefully put his three-cornered hat
on the deck in front of him. Then
he stood on his head with his boots
waving in the air. Ruby handed him
the cup of water to drink and held up
his long beard, which had flopped
down over his face.

"Oh, and I forgot," Ruby said. "You're supposed to sing too."

Ruby used her free hand to pull on her plaits for luck. The captain started to sing and drink while Harry and Olly held on to one leg each to steady him.

"Ahoy ... *gulp* ... pirates ... *gulp* ... sailin' the seas ... *gulp*," he started. "Yo, ho ... *gulp, cough, splutter, HIC!*" Redbeard hiccupped so hard that he fell over and squashed his captain's hat. "Avast ye ... *hic* ... no good ... *hic* ... landlubbers!" he shouted as he got up from the floor and put on his flattened hat.

Harry stepped forward. "Captain,

79

we're sorry that didn't work. But we do need to stop you from hiccupping before the ship gets even more lost."

Captain Redbeard grew even more red in the face than he had been before. "Captain's orders ... *hic* ... stop hiccupping!" he shouted, and fell on to the deck with the effort.

Ruby turned to Olly. "What's he doing?" she asked.

"I'm pretty sure he's ordering his hiccups to stop hiccupping," Olly said.

"Avast ye . . . *hic* . . . hiccups!" the captain said.

"I don't think they're listening to him," Ruby said. "And if we can't stop his hiccups, we could all be lost on this ship forever!"

Chapter Seven
Puppy on the Plank

"Captain, I don't think you can order hiccups to stop," Harry said, helping the captain up. "I read about how your body controls hiccupping on its own, like making your heart beat. You see, your diaphragm contracts and pushes up air, which makes your vocal chords close and creates that hiccupping sound," Harry explained.

Ruby saw that Olly, Patch and
Captain Redbeard all had the same
confused expression on their faces.

Harry blushed and tried again.
"Sorry, a diaphragm's like a little
trampoline in your body bouncing air
up that catches in your throat."

The captain nodded.

"So all you have to do is stop the air," Harry said.

"I get it. Hold your breath," Ruby added.

"I hope this works," Olly said, crossing his fingers.

Captain Redbeard held his breath until his whiskered cheeks seemed ready to pop. *A puffer fish, that's what he looks like*, thought Ruby, as she blew out her cheeks as well and pushed out her lips to appear more fishy.

Puddle beat his tail in time on the deck of the ship while Harry counted. "Eight golden doubloons, nine golden doubloons, ten . . ."

"Aaaaah," Captain Redbeard ran out of puff and gasped for air.

Everyone on the pirate ship fell silent and waited to see if the captain was cured.

"*Hic!*" went the captain.

Puddle suddenly ran forward and started yapping at the captain.

"Do you see another whirlpool, Puddle?" Olly asked.

Puddle growled at Captain Redbeard and the captain growled back at Puddle, between hiccups.

Making the captain even madder isn't going to help, Ruby thought. "Puddle – don't be naughty!" she called. He was running around the captain's legs and barking.

Captain Redbeard shouted out to Olly and Patch. "Stop that ... *hic* ... crazy wee dog ... *hic!*"

The pirates tried to get Puddle to chase a stick or eat a biscuit, but the puppy just kept running round the captain. It almost seemed like Puddle was trying to steer Captain Redbeard towards the side of the ship.

"What's up with Puddle?" Harry whispered to Ruby.

"Thar headin' fer the plank!" shouted Patch.

Ruby saw that he was right. Puddle was backing the captain on to the wooden plank that jutted from the side of the ship.

"Let me . . . *hic* . . . be," shouted Redbeard. He was soon standing at the end of the plank with Puddle yapping at his toes.

Harry whispered, "Puddle could really scare someone like that."

"Ah-ha!" said Ruby. "Puddle's trying to scare the hiccups out of the captain. I really hope this works." She had her fingers crossed and her toes crossed too inside her wellies.

Captain Redbeard peered down at the rolling ocean waves. "Help, me hearties! I can't swim!" he shouted. Puddle sat up and wagged his tail.

Ruby clapped her hands, "You clever puppy," she said.

The captain shouted to Ruby and Harry. "If ye thinks yer little dog be so clever, then we'll see how clever he be walkin' the plank himself."

The other pirates stared at him in disbelief.

"What ye be starin' at, ye sea dogs?" Redbeard asked. "You'll all be walking the plank if ye don't show yer Cap'n . . ." Then he suddenly stopped and stroked his beard.

Olly smiled and Patch let out a belly laugh and slapped his thigh. "Well, blow me down," he said.

Ruby stepped forward and picked up Puddle. Puddle licked her face.

"Captain, Puddle has cured your hiccups."

Chapter Eight
Sea-Faring Friends

"He's scared them out of you, Captain,"
Ruby said, taking Redbeard's hand as
he stepped off the plank.

"Hornswaggle! Nothing scares
Redbeard!" The captain laughed and
leaned down to ruffle Puddle's ears.
"Arrrr, ye old sea dog!" he said.
"Ye'd make a fierce wee pirate, ye
really would."

Olly tapped Redbeard on the shoulder. "Captain? We're still way off course, and we do need to head to shore for supplies."

"Maybe I can help," said Harry, taking out his compass from his pocket. Olly fetched the ship's maps and navigating equipment. Ruby held the compass, and Harry plotted a course to take them to shore.

"Thanks for all your help," Olly said to Ruby and Harry.

Puddle pounced on the ship's wheel and ran over the handles, making it spin like a giant hamster wheel.

The ship jerked like it had when the captain had hiccupped. Puddle leapt down and wagged his tail.

"Puddle, you are the naughtiest puppy ever," Ruby said, smiling.

"No, Puddle's the naughtiest pirate puppy," Olly said.

"Full ahead, me hearties!" Captain Redbeard shouted to his crew. "Olly me lad," the captain added, "You take the wheel. Captain's orders. Good to practice. Ye may be a captain yerself one day."

Olly beamed and Patch patted him on the back. "Aye, aye, Captain," Olly said.

When Captain Redbeard leaned down to give Puddle a stroke on the head, Puddle jumped up and gave the pirate captain a lick on his red-bearded cheek.

Then Puddle started running in circles around the cousins.

"I guess it's time we found our way home too, Puddle," Ruby said.

Ruby felt tingly as she gazed up at the sails. They seemed to go fuzzy and spin around. *This must be what it feels like to be in a washing machine with white sheets tumbling around you,* Ruby thought. She and Harry could

see the pirates waving goodbye to them through the haze.

"Goodbye, everyone!" Ruby shouted.

Harry cleared his throat. "Farewell, me hearties!" he called across the deck.

Ruby laughed. "You're a proper pirate now," she said.

The pirates and the ship faded away, and Ruby, Harry and Puddle landed with a huge *splash* right in the middle of Grandad's pond.

"Puddle, I think you went a bit off course too," Harry said.

Puddle paddled to the muddy bank and bounded on to the grass. He turned to the cousins, woofed, and dashed through the reeds out of sight. Ruby and Harry helped pull each other out. Ruby was starting to wring out her plaits when she saw something lying by Harry's ship, which was floating by a clump of rushes. She ran over to it, her wet plaits thumping against her shoulders, and picked it up.

"A pirate hat!" she said, putting it on. "Ahoy, matey!" she shouted to Harry. "I think I've had enough of being a queen. Let's be pirates!" She picked up a reed and waved it above her head like a floppy sword. "Arrr, have at ye," she shouted. "Let's find buried treasure or raid Grandad's biscuit jar!"

Harry smiled as he raced over and picked up his model ship. Suddenly his body shuddered and he dropped the ship in the pond with a *splash!*

"Ahoy, there," Ruby said. "You don't want to break your ship."

Harry turned to face Ruby. "What's the matter?" she asked.

Harry smiled. "I've . . . *hic* . . . got the . . . *hic* . . . hiccups!"

Can't wait to find out
what Puddle will do next?
Then read on! Here is the first
chapter from Puddle's eighth
adventure, Animal Antics . . .

Animal Antics

"Aha!" cried Ruby, picking up the magnifying glass on Grandad's desk. "Now Chief Inspector Ruby, the great Animal Detective, can search for clues to solve the Mystery of the Missing Platypus!"

Her cousin Harry looked at her over the top of his glasses.

"You don't need a magnifying

glass to find your toy duck-billed platypus," he told Ruby. "You just need to remember where you left it."

Harry turned over the cushion on Grandad's chair. "Nothing under here," he said.

"I remember bringing him into Grandad's study when I was looking for a book to read ..." Ruby held the magnifying glass to her eye and scanned the books in Grandad's bookcase. She could see her fingerprints in a thin layer of dust where she'd taken out a book, but there was no sign of Teddy, her toy duck-billed platypus.

"Perhaps I put Teddy down

somewhere," she murmured.

Ruby's plaits swung as she dropped to her knees to search under the desk. Her tummy did a somersault. There was a faint line of muddy paw prints on the study floor. Puppy paw prints!

"Harry, look!" she cried. "Puddle's been here!"

"Let me see." Harry took the magnifying glass and knelt down to examine the prints.

"They're still damp!" he exclaimed. A big smile spread across his face. "It must be raining again."

Ruby clapped her hands in delight. Whenever it rained, the little puppy arrived and they went on amazing adventures together.

"Where did Puddle go?" she wondered aloud. "He's disappeared, like Teddy."

"Let's hunt for Teddy later," Harry said. "Right now, we have to crack the Case of the Disappearing Puppy!" He pushed his glasses up his nose. "I've been reading a book called *Whodunnit*," he said. "It's all about how detectives solve mysteries. These paw prints are clues. We can track them."

Harry set off across the study floor on his hands and knees, holding the magnifying glass above the faint paw prints.

Ruby was close behind Harry as they followed the trail under Grandad's chair, out of the study, along the hallway and into the kitchen. The back door of the cottage was ajar and the muddy prints led outside.

Ruby and Harry jumped to their feet and pulled on their wellies.

"Quick!" Harry said. "We have to follow Puddle's prints before the rain washes them away."

"They're heading for Grandad's vegetable patch," Ruby said as they dashed up the garden path. The rain was falling harder now and the paw prints were already fading.

"Puddle, where are you?" Ruby called.

Nearby, one of Grandad's lettuces started to shake. Ruby stared at it. A little white muzzle with a black rubbery nose was poking out from the middle. The lettuce leaves surrounded it like a bright green mane.

"Puddle!" Ruby laughed. "You look just like a little green lion."

"Woof!" Puddle barked. He leapt out of the lettuce, sending leaves flying everywhere, and licked Ruby's nose.

"Yuck!" Ruby spluttered.

"There goes one of Grandad's

prize-winning lettuces," Harry groaned.

Puddle ran up to a big puddle that had formed in a dip in the path. He slowly circled it then turned back to Ruby and Harry, wagging his tail.

"Woof! Woof!" he barked. "WOOF!" And he leapt into the puddle and disappeared in a shower of raindrops!

Ruby glanced at Harry and tugged on her plaits for luck. "Adventure time!" she squealed as they jumped in after the naughty little puppy.

***

To find out what happens next, get your copy of ANIMAL ANTICS today!

Magic Mayhem

Ruby and Harry are amazed to find themselves in a medieval castle...

...when Puddle takes them on their latest adventure! They meet a magician's apprentice who is in deep trouble. He's lost his spell book. Can Puddle save the day?

Find out in MAGIC MAYHEM...

Animal Antics

Join Puddle, Ruby and Harry
at the Safari Rescue Park!

All the animals
have problems they
need to overcome
before they can be
released into the
wild. Will Puddle
be able to help the
monkey who is
afraid of heights?

Find out in ANIMAL ANTICS…

Puddle
the naughtiest puppy

Christmas
Snow Puppy

Go on a festive adventure with Ruby,
Harry and Puddle!

The children find
themselves in a
beautiful winter
wonderland.
Can they get
through the snow
to the big winter
festival on time?

Find out in CHRISTMAS SNOW PUPPY…
Coming soon!

Star of the School

Join Puddle, Ruby and Harry on their new adventure in the Wild West!

Lil the littlest cowgirl is told she is too small to join the cowboy school. But with Puddle's help, can she prove herself by catching Outlaw Pete?

Find out in STAR OF THE SCHOOL…

Puddle the naughtiest puppy

Holiday Musical

Go on an amazing Hollywood adventure
with Ruby, Harry and Puddle!

The children are
thrilled when they
get to star in a new
movie. But the
director thinks
Puddle has stolen
the script! How can
Puddle show he's
not to blame?

Find out in HOLIDAY MUSICAL...

Play Time

Hi, it's Ruby and Harry again with Puddle the puppy! Didn't you think our latest adventure was fantastic fun?

Dogs Trust, the UK's largest dog charity, are here with us again to help us find out about real dogs. Today we will be learning about the importance of play time.

Just like us, dogs love to play, and it is a good way of keeping them fit and healthy. There are lots of doggy toys available. Some of these can be used to help you train your dog, and others are just for fun!

Always remember, Puddle is a magical dog, while real dogs and puppies are living animals who need a lot of care, love and attention.

Play time rules:

- Although we all love playing, you must always play with your own toys and your dog must play with his own.
- When playing with dogs you should always have an adult there to keep you both safe.
- There are lots of different games you can play with your dog — can you think of any? Fetch is a great game — simply throw a ball or toy for your dog and let them fetch it. (In the garden, of course!)
- Sometimes your dog will be tired and might not want to play — if this happens you must leave him alone.

Congratulations – you understand that play time is as important to a dog as it is to you and me! See you next time when we will be talking about taking your dog to the vet.

Remember, "A dog is for life, not just for Christmas®" Dogs Trust has 18 Rehoming Centres around the UK and Ireland. To find out more please go to: www.dogstrust.org.uk

For more fun and games please go to: www.learnwithdogs.co.uk

Mystery Circles!

A piece of a character is shown in each circle. Look at the clues and see if you can work out who is shown in each picture.

1. I have a bushy beard and a fierce temper.

2. I'm the youngest first mate on the high seas.

3. I nearly fell from a ladder on the ship.

4. I'm a friendly old pirate.

Pirate Puzzler!

Look carefully at the picture of Captain Redbeard below. One of the pictures on the opposite page matches it exactly. Can you work out which one it is?

Answers on the next page

Answers to puzzles:

Mystery Circles: 1. Captain Redbeard; 2. Olly; 3. Ruby; 4. Patch

Pirate Puzzler: C is the exact match

For more magical adventures, come and play with Puddle at

www.puddlethepuppy.com

Use this special code to get extra special games and free stuff at puddlethepuppy.com

PIRATE HAT